Twelve Iron Sandals

TWELVE
IRON SANDALS
And Other Czechoslovak Tales

by VÍT HOŘEJŠ

illustrated by JIM SPANFELLER

Prentice-Hall, Inc.
Englewood Cliffs, New Jersey

Printed in the United States of America   ·J

Prentice-Hall International, Inc., London
Prentice-Hall of Australia, Pty. Ltd., Sydney
Prentice-Hall Canada, Inc., Toronto
Prentice-Hall Hispanoamericana, S.A., Mexico
Prentice-Hall of India Private Ltd., New Delhi
Prentice-Hall of Japan, Inc., Tokyo
Prentice-Hall of Southeast Asia Pte. Ltd., Singapore
Whitehall Books Limited, Wellington, New Zealand
Editora Prentice-Hall do Brasil LTDA., Rio de Janeiro

10 9 8 7 6 5 4 3 2 1

Book design by Constance Ftera

Library of Congress Cataloging in Publication Data

Hořejš, Vít.
    Twelve iron sandals and other Czechoslovak tales.

    Summary: A prince's release from a nocturnal spell is
endangered by his wife's disobedience unless she wears
out twelve iron sandals, in the first of these seven
Czech folk and fairy tales.
    1. Fairy tales—Czechoslovakia. [1. Fairy tales.
2. Folklore—Czechoslovakia] I. Spanfeller, James J.,
1930-   ill. II. Title.
PZ8.H782Tw   1985   398.2'09437   84-22272

To my father, Jaromír Hořejš

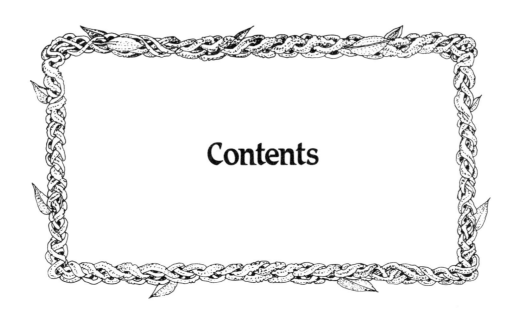

Contents

Twelve Iron Sandals

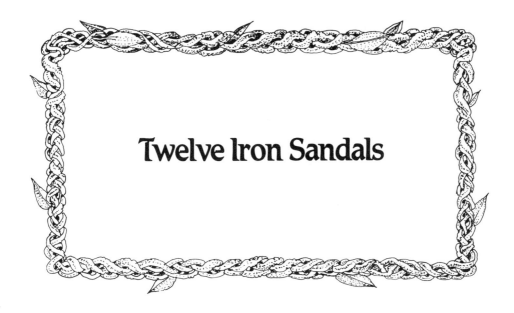

Twelve Iron Sandals

ONCE UPON A TIME, there was a king who had three daughters. The two elder ones were married, but the youngest one could not choose a husband. She was beautiful and clever, and she didn't think much of the throngs of kings, princes, and high nobility who came as suitors.

One day a young man unknown to her court presented himself to the Princess. He was handsome and splendidly dressed and the presents he gave to the King and to the Princesses surpassed anything the other suitors could offer. Immediately, the young woman felt a sensation that she had never experienced before. Still, she waited for a week before she said yes, she wanted to marry the man.

At that moment, the young knight asked to be left alone with the Princess for a short while. When everybody left, he told her,

"My love, I have to reveal a secret to you: I am a King of a faraway country, ten times more powerful than your father. However, I can spend only the daylight hours with you. At night I must be alone, prisoner of the spell cast upon me by an evil magician because I rejected his daughter's hand in marriage. Yet I assure you the spell will not last forever. One day we will travel to take possession of my kingdom."

"I am prepared to endure any hardship for love of you," said the Princess, "and I will be patient if the spell should last to the end of our days."

They married when spring turned to summer. Everybody envied the Princess for her handsome, wise, and enormously rich husband. The magnificence of the wedding feast is still told in legends and sung by minstrels of many countries.

As the days passed, everybody grew to like and admire the young King even more. Compliments rained on the Princess's ears, giving her great pleasure.

The days became weeks and the weeks stretched into months. The Princess became weary of listening to compliments about her beloved, a man whose nights she could not share. In the middle of the most exciting pastime, the young King would get up and leave. He would lock himself in his chamber until dawn and the Princess was left to her tears, alone in her bed which was too large and cold to embrace her loneliness.

One day the two lovers were so deeply immersed in a game of charades that the Princess forgot about her predicament. It wasn't until dusk that she remembered, yet she was sure her husband wouldn't leave this time. But as if he could read her thoughts, the King got up again and left the chamber to lock himself in his own room. The Princess tiptoed behind him and looked through the keyhole. To her amazement, her husband put on a scaly green

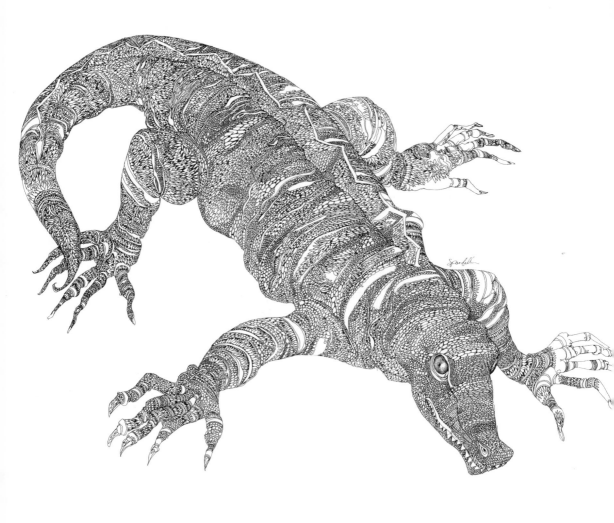

skin and became a huge lizard. In that likeness he coiled in front of the fireplace, sighed deeply, and went to sleep.

Days, weeks, and months passed again. The days were most enjoyable for the royal couple, the nights were most dreary. One afternoon, the two were again deeply engrossed, this time in a game of chess. As evening approached, the Princess grew distraught, and finally she sat silent and motionless, not answering the King's caresses and entreaties.

Shortly before dusk she got up and ran out of the room. The King followed apace. To his surprise, she led him to his own bedroom. There, before he could stop her, she snatched the lizard skin from the wall and tossed it into the fireplace. In the flames the skin coiled into a tight knot, then sizzled and was burnt in a minute.

The King sighed deeply and said, "It would have been better if you had kept your patience for another month. For in that short time, my spell would have been over. Now I am at the mercy of the evil magician's vengeful daughter—lost to you forever. For to find me you would have to wear out twelve iron sandals, break twelve iron staves, and eat twelve iron loaves of bread."

With these words, the King disappeared.

The Princess dispatched messengers to the remotest parts of the world to find a trace of her husband. She promised rewards and inquired of all travelers, neighbors, friends, enemies, and even the sea pirates. All in vain. Finally she saw there was no other way: she alone had to search for her husband.

Remembering his words, the Princess had twelve iron sandals made, twelve iron staves, and twelve iron loaves of bread. She was bent over under the heavy load. It took years before she wore out the first pair of iron sandals and broke the first iron staff. The hard loaf of iron bread seemed to have no end. Many times she felt desperate as she walked through wilderness, deserts, and marshlands. Often she fell under her burden and thought she would never get up again.

Yet after much suffering, the twelfth pair of iron sandals was wearing thin, the twelfth iron staff was bent, and there was only a

mouthful of iron bread left in her knapsack. It was at that time that she arrived at her husband's kingdom. She camped in front of his palace. But the King never came out of the palace gate. Good people told her that the kingdom had been taken over by the wicked Queen. Nobody knew where she came from, nobody remembered a wedding, but there she was, governing with an iron fist. Ever since the King returned from a long journey abroad, he seemed ill and had no say in the Queen's decisions.

The Princess sat down in front of the palace gate and set her golden necklace, the King's present, in front of her as if for sale. The Queen passed by and asked what the price was.

"The necklace was a gift from someone very dear to me," said the Princess. "No one on earth can pay the price it's worth to me. But I will give it to you if you allow me to spend one night in the King's bedroom."

The Queen tried to haggle, she threatened and cajoled, but the Princess wouldn't be moved.

Finally the Queen gave in. She took the necklace and with a cruel smile she led the girl to the King's bedroom.

"I hope you'll enjoy yourself," she said unpleasantly as she let the Princess into the darkened chamber.

The King lay on a large canopy bed covered with silken sheets, pale and silent. Instead of joy, the Princess was seized with pain at the look of him, for his body was pierced with thousands of needles from head to toe. Only the faint twitching of his wounded eyelids proved he wasn't dead.

The Princess began immediately to remove the needles from his body. Wherever she pulled them out, his skin regained its healthy color. She could follow the King's breathing now, and as she freed his chest of the needles, his breathing became more and more regular. Ignoring the pain as her nimble fingers were pricked with needles, she kept at her task. The blood dripped from her fingers, yet she kept talking to the King in a soothing voice, recalling the blissful time they had spent together and the cruel years of her pilgrimage.

Only his face and one hand were left to be cleaned of needles when the door of the chamber flew open and the Queen's cracked voice bade her leave.

"And never come back," the Queen croaked, "unless you have presents more precious than your necklace."

Without a word, the stunned Princess pointed with her torn fingers to her ears. She had most magnificent earrings, of such fine work and studded with such crystal-clear gems that they far surpassed her necklace in value.

The deal was shortly made: the Princess wouldn't give her earrings for anything but another night in the King's bedroom.

She couldn't sleep the whole day with excitement and with pain, for her fingers grew swollen as the hundreds of needle wounds festered. In the evening, the Queen palmed the earrings and shoved the Princess into the King's chamber.

Dumbfounded, the Princess saw that his body was covered with even more needles than the night before. She had toiled and suffered for nothing.

Yet she immediately sat down to pull the needles out of the poor King's body. She felt excruciating pain in her swollen fingers, ten times worse than the night before. She worked feverishly, almost fainting from pain. At midnight there were only the eyelids left, pierced with hundreds of needles. She couldn't get hold of the tiny needles, her swollen bleeding fingertips slipping and driving them even deeper into her husband's eyes.

Yet she wouldn't give up. One by one, in terrible pain, she pulled the tiny needles out. There were hardly a dozen left when she saw that the night had paled behind the windows. Horrorstricken, she pulled out another needle, and another . . . Too late!

The door creaked behind her and the shrill laugh clanged in her ears.

"Now, get out," hissed the Queen finally, "get out of here before I get angry!"

With bent head, the Princess stumbled to the door, cradling her shredded fingers. Then, without a word, she extended her crippled left hand before the Queen's eyes.

"This ring is my last possession," she said. "The largest diamond itself is worth more than the whole of your palace. I'll give you the ring for one last night in the King's bedroom."

The wicked woman's eyes shone with greed.

"All right," she said, "agreed. But under one condition. You have offended me long enough with your impudent requests. No woman can go unpunished for spending night after night with my husband. You can have the third night with him, but tomorrow you will be beheaded."

The girl shivered at the thought but there was nothing more she could lose. Tears streamed from her eyes and she staggered in pain as she pulled the ring from her lacerated finger.

Again, for pain and fear she couldn't close her eyes all day, though her whole body cried for rest. As she walked toward the palace that night, she hurt her foot on a sharp stone. She looked and saw that she had worn a hole in her last iron sandal. She remembered the last piece of iron bread and bit into the hard crumb. To her amazement the bread seemed tasty for the first time on her long journey, and as she swallowed it, she felt strength returning to her tired limbs and the pain lessening in her fingers. However, as hard as she leaned on her iron staff, she couldn't break it.

This time she was prepared for seeing the needles in her beloved husband's skin, yet she swayed, for their number had doubled once again. Without delay she sat down to work. She worked ever faster and faster, heedless of pain and tiredness. She felt confident she would succeed this time, but the thought of the last iron staff remained like a black cloud over her head.

There was only one needle left in each of her husband's eyelids when the key creaked in the bedroom door. She pulled one needle out, not daring to look through the window, where the pale dawn was spreading its crumpled wings.

One of the King's eyes opened. He didn't move or say a word. Yet the Princess thought that one look was worth dying for.

The shrill unpleasant laugh filled the room. "Guards! Seize the intruder!" screeched the wicked Queen.

The Princess held tight to the last needle. She could not extricate it from the King's eye. The guards grabbed her. But as they snatched her up from the bedside, the needle at last came away in her hand.

"Stop! Let her go!" The King's voice rang young and resolute through the room. He jumped out of his bed, seized the last iron staff, and broke it in two.

"Take this witch instead," he ordered, pointing at the Queen. "She no longer has power over me."

The astonished guards obeyed gladly. The wicked woman, the daughter of the evil magician, was burned at the stake the very next Sunday, while the young pair rejoiced at their happy reunion. They spent day after day recounting their love and the suffering of these long years. And if they haven't died, they live in bliss to this day.

The Fisherman's Clever Daughter

ONCE THERE WAS A BEAUTIFUL TOWN in a beautiful faraway country. The good King of that country decided to give a present to his favorite town: he gave the city councilmen enough money to build a new town hall.

The town hall was built of white stone. It had Greek columns, Moorish arches, Byzantine porticos, and a gilded statue of the Mayor killing a lion. It was furnished with equal care and taste. To show their gratitude to the King, the city councilmen decided to inscribe this sentence on the front arch:

"We Live Without Worries."

The whole town came to the opening celebration. Everyone was excited, for the King himself was to be there. However, when the good monarch saw the inscription on the building, his face contorted as if he had bitten into a rotten apple. He suddenly commanded his driver to turn his golden carriage and left the beautiful town without saying a single word.

The alarmed city councilmen followed their good King, but they didn't dare to approach him until he stopped at an inn to change his exhausted horses for fresh ones.

"You boast about living without a worry. That couldn't be said about me. But I'll take care of that," the King said. "I'll make you worry. Answer this question: 'What is the sweetest, strongest, and most valuable thing in the world?' If you don't find the solution for the riddle within a week, the whole city council is going to be executed—each one in a different way. I'll spend the whole night figuring out something special for the mayor."

The councilmen returned to their new town hall and immediately started deliberations.

"Why, it's easy," said the tavernkeeper. "The sweetest thing in the world is my wine."

"No," jumped up the beekeeper, "not that rotgut. The sweetest thing in the world is my honey and the strongest is the bear who will split a hundred-year-old tree to get at it."

"Ridiculous," yelled the butcher, "the strongest is a young bull and the most valuable is the chest of gold in my cellar."

"Nonsense," cried another one, "the sweetest is the voice of my—" and so on and so forth. They promised a huge reward to anybody who could come up with the right answer. They argued for six days. Each day at sunset they sent a messenger to the King with the new answer. But none were on the mark.

On the seventh day the councilmen and the whole town were dejected, exhausted, tired of royal riddles and tired of royal gifts. That day a poor fisherman presented himself humbly to the council.

"Excuse me, high councilmen," he said, "but my daughter's

been on my back for the last week saying she knows the answer to the King's riddle."

"That's the solution," snapped the Mayor, awakening suddenly out of his stupor. "I'm sure he's got the right answer. Let him go to the King as our messenger. Not only that; I offer you my resignation and I nominate this man as our next mayor."

The astonished councilmen didn't want to let the Mayor get away so easily, but they were really too tired. Before the fisherman knew what was happening, he was elected Mayor, on his way to the capital, and if his daughter's wit failed, on his way to capital punishment.

By the time the poor man was introduced into the royal chamber, his knees were killing him from banging against each other because his legs were shaking so much.

"Well, what is your answer?" asked the King, who had to raise his voice to be heard over the rattling of the fisherman's teeth.

"D-D-D—Dreamhopelife," blurted the fisherman. "I mean, a dream is the sweetest thing in the world, hope is the strongest, and life the most valuable."

"You're right, Mayor," the King said slowly, looking for some way to catch him out. "But you, Mayor, couldn't possibly have come up with the right answer. I'll be Mayor if you did. Who helped you?"

"My daughter, sire," said the astonished fisherman-Mayor. "Lenka is her name."

"If she's so clever," the King said, "I have a little task for her. Here, take this yarn. I want her to weave me a nice shirt."

The King handed the fisherman-Mayor two red threads, each about four inches long. The poor man walked home with a heavy heart, while the good King tried to figure out some sort of punishment for both the father and Lenka.

But the girl just laughed when she heard the task.

"Go back to the palace," she told her father, "and take these two matches to the King. Tell him to build me a loom with the matches, then I'll weave his shirt without delay."

Afraid to offend the King with Lenka's daring answer, the fisherman could hardly speak. But the King was amused.

"All right," he said, "but I have something else for her. Here, take this leaking pot to your daughter. Ask her to darn the pot for me. But the work has to be done neatly, not a stitch should show on the bottom. Now be gone, I have something important to think about."

"That's quite easy," Lenka told her frightened father. "But first you have to take the pot back. Ask the King to turn it inside out and then I'll do the darning."

When the King heard her answer, he invited the clever maiden to his palace.

"But," he said, "she must come neither during the day nor at night, neither riding nor afoot, neither dressed nor naked, and she must bring me a present that is no present.

"Is that clear, Mayor? In the meantime I'll think out some proper punishment for both of you should she fail."

There was nothing else for the befuddled fisherman to do but to go home and relate the King's kind invitation to his daughter.

"Do not worry, father," said Lenka, "there's nothing easier."

On the appointed day, she went to the palace at three in the morning, when the night was over but the day hadn't dawned yet. Wrapped only in an old fishnet, Lenka sat on a goat: she was riding, but with her bare feet she touched the ground. She carried the present for the King in her closed fist. In the audience room she opened her hand—and the bee she had been holding flew out the window.

The King liked her attire and he had to admit that she had fulfilled the task.

"I want to marry you, fair maiden," he said. "But you have to promise one thing. Under no circumstances are you to interfere with my royal decisions. I am the King here. If you should break your word, you'll go back to your hovel with no more to put on than your fishing net."

Lenka promised and they married. For years she kept her promise, avoiding any talk about royal matters. But one day, while the King was away hunting, a peasant came to ask for help. He had stayed overnight at an inn with his cart, he said, and that night his mare had given birth to a colt. The colt wandered around the stable, and in the morning a broom peddler found the colt next to his wheelbarrow loaded with brooms. To the peasant's dismay, the peddler now claimed the colt was his, born from his wheelbarrow. They had brought their case to the King and he had awarded the colt to the broom peddler.

"Here's what you have to do," the Queen said, and she explained her plan to the peasant.

"But please," she said, "don't ever tell the King that I gave you advice."

On his way home, the King met the peasant sitting on the road. The peasant was casting a fishnet in the dirt, pulling the net in and casting it again.

"What are you doing, fool?" asked the King.

"Fishing, my lord."

"But there are no fish in the dirt."

"Why, I'd say so, my lord, but in these times when wheelbarrows can bear colts, I surely hope to find some fish in the dirt. Why, it's deep enough."

The King recognized the man and realized that his judgment had been wrong.

"Serves me right," the King said. "I should have awarded you the colt. But tell me, you didn't have such smart ideas when you pleaded your case. Who helped you? Who gave you advice?"

The good man didn't want to say, but the King asked in such a kind manner and with such insistence that he finally wheedled the truth out of the peasant.

"It was the Queen, my lord," he said.

Back in the castle, the King called his clever wife.

"You have broken your promise," he said, "and now I must fulfill mine. Tomorrow you'll put on your fishing net again and leave the castle. All your belongings, all my gifts to you, all your jewels and clothes are to be left behind. I want, however, to reward you for being a good wife. You can take one thing with you, the one thing in the castle you like the most."

The Queen said, "As your Majesty commands. But, please, I would like you to share one last dinner with me tonight."

The King agreed. The Queen herself prepared a delicious meal. She didn't eat or drink too much, but she poured glass after glass of the best wine for the King. To the last glass she added a sleeping potion that sent the King fast into his dreams.

When he was sound asleep, she called a trusted servant and with his help carried the King to her bedroom. She put the sleeping King into a big chest that she had prepared, and early in the morning she left the castle with the chest tied onto a cart dispatched by the chamberlain.

It wasn't until noon that the King woke up in the fisherman's cottage. At first he couldn't understand where he was. Then he began calling for help, for he thought he had been kidnapped. But the clever fisherman's daughter told him, "You allowed me to

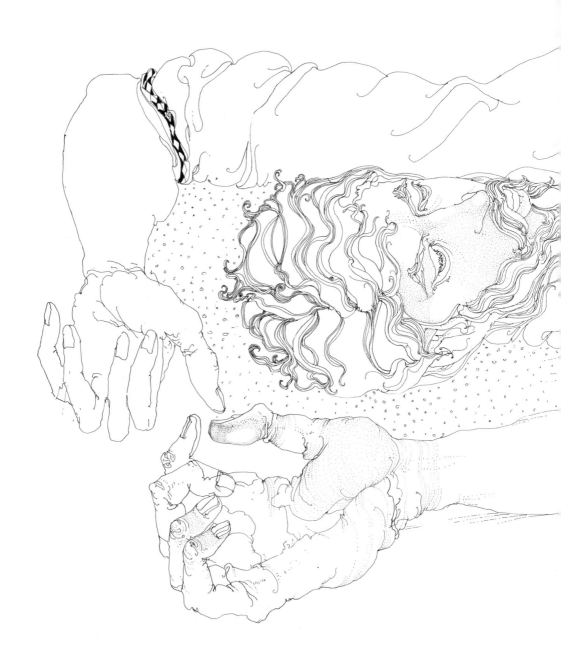

take home the thing in the castle that I liked the most and I didn't like anything better than you."

The King didn't know what to answer so he just frowned. He frowned and frowned and frowned and then he started laughing.

"You have outwitted me again," he said, "and you have taught me a lesson about love, too. Will you return to the castle with me?"

His wife, however, insisted on spending some time with her father, so the King stayed with them in the cottage for two more days. When they finally returned to the castle, the Queen was allowed to take part in all the government proceedings. And never had the King a counselor more shrewd than the fisherman's clever daughter.

The Wheelmaker's Son

THERE WAS ONCE A WHEELMAKER who had three sons: Koloděj, Matěj, and Kuděj. When the oldest one came of age, he decided to go out in the world to pick up some wisdom wherever they grew it. In a napkin he wrapped a provision of *buchtas*, the kind of sweet rolls that Czech mothers make, filled with plum butter or white cheese and raisins. Then he parted from his parents and brothers and went on his way.

Koloděj felt cheerful. He sang to make marching easier. He paid no attention to the people he met along the road but kept singing as he went. And as he sang, he thought about his profession. He knew he was a good craftsman, oh yes, the best of the three brothers. And he was content.

Note: Koloděj is pronounced *kolodyey*; Matěj is *matyey*; Kuděj is *koudyey*.

As evening approached and his limbs began to fill with tiredness, Koloděj stopped at the side of the road to rest.

"Why don't I make myself a wagon," he thought. "Maybe I could even buy a horse, if I find a cheap one."

He set about working on a wagon.

He was just carving an axle when a tall, thin old man appeared in front of him. Who knows where he came from?

"God help you, young man!" he greeted Koloděj. But the young wheelmaker didn't answer.

The old man went on to ask what he was doing.

Koloděj replied, "I am a wheelmaker by profession, so I want to make myself a wagon, to spare myself the darned walking."

But the old man said, "My son, this wagon won't budge an inch." And off he went.

Koloděj didn't give a hoot about where the old man had gone and he went on working. By sunset he had a wagon ready and decided to try it out. He set it on the road and gave it a push. But try as hard as he could, the wagon would not move. Not an inch.

When Koloděj saw there was no way to budge the wagon, he broke it into pieces, sat down on the edge of the field, and ate all of his rolls. Then he slept under a big tree and in the morning he set out for home.

Now it was the turn of the second son. Matěj also packed a bunch of *buchtas* and a piece of bacon and took off. He, too, felt cheerful and full of life. The birds were singing way up in the sky, the earth smelled invitingly damp, and the sun shone as never before.

As he walked, what did he suddenly see in the ditch: a wheel here, an axle over on the other side, and a pole a dozen yards farther down the road. Without thinking twice about it he started to gather the pieces and fit them together.

"Who knows," he thought, "maybe I'll find a cheap horse to drive me around. And if not, at least I can ride down the hill."

The wagon was just about ready to go when the thin old man happened along.

"God help you, young wheelmaker!"

Matěj went on working.

"And what is it you're working at?" the old man asked.

"You have three guesses," Matěj replied. "If that's not enough, I will help you. See: a wheel, and another, four wheels, two axles, a pole—what could that be? Perhaps a wagon? You've got it! Aren't you clever. I am a wheelmaker, this is a wagon. The wheelmaker will sit on the wagon, you see, and ride along, spare the soles of his shoes."

But the old man told him, too, "You could spare yourself the trouble, this wagon won't budge an inch."

The young man didn't really hear him that well. He went back to work, and in a little while the wagon was ready to go. But go it did not. Matěj could push and pull as much as he wanted, but the wagon stood as if it had grown roots. The wheelmaker's second son grew angry. He took the wagon apart, ate all his provisions, and went to sleep under the bushes. He got up at noon and returned home the way he had come.

There was only the third son left, the youngest.

"You've tried your luck," he said. "You were both out in the world. Now it's my turn to try."

The wheelmaker's wife baked him plum *buchtas*, wrapped them in a napkin, and the youth set off.

The sun was setting when he got to the place where both his brothers had worked on the wagon without success. Well, what do you think Kudĕj's profession was: he was a wheelmaker, for a change. He decided to fix the wagon and ride along a little. He knew, although he was the youngest, that his journey would be a long one.

Kuděj didn't waste time, and before the first star appeared, the old man walked up to him and said, "God help you, young man!"

"So he may, good old man," answered Kuděj. "And where are you bound so late at night?"

"Not too far away, my son, not far. But I am so very old, my legs are not worth much anymore. I am so tired that I ache all over."

The young wheelmaker took pity on the old traveler. He invited him to sit down and pulled the plum *buchtas* out of his bundle. They shared the supper under the stars. When they were both full, the thin old man asked Kuděj what he was working on.

"You know, good old man, the journey may be a long one, so I am putting together this wagon that I found broken in the ditch. The wood is good, so the wagon should ride all right."

"Of course it will," the old man told him, "but I must first give you a piece of advice, or the wagon won't budge an inch. Take this twig from me. When you get in the wagon, strike it with the twig. The more you hit, the faster the wagon will go. Remember well my words, and whomever you meet on the road, take him with you."

Then the old man went on his way and Kuděj was alone. Glad to have been given such good advice, he jumped in the wagon, swung the twig once, and the wagon started to move. He swung twice and the wagon sped along smoothly. He swung the twig for the third and fourth times: the wagon spurted forward in a cloud of dust.

Before you could say "Nincompoop ordered a half kookaburra on rye," he was entering the next village. By the first house stood a raggedy beggar with enormously long legs. Kuděj remembered the old man's words and invited the beggar to sit in the wagon. And off they went. They streaked through villages like lightning, they enjoyed the ride so much. At a crossroads they met another wanderer. This one had three golden balls in his hands. Kuděj invited him to join the party and off they went again.

Then they met a third traveler, but he was really a weird one. He was rather small but enormously fat and his mouth, you should have seen it—if he hadn't had ears, it would have stretched around his whole head. That's how large it was. Kuděj offered him a seat in the wagon and off they went, raising dust.

They rode the whole night and day. The next evening they stopped at a tavern to have dinner. While they were eating, the tavernkeeper's daughter looked out her window and saw the golden balls in the wagon. She wanted to steal them, but the moment she touched the balls, they stuck to her fingers—staying as if glued to the wagon at the same time. She pulled and shook her hand, she nearly tore her fingers off, but no, she was trapped.

The four travelers finished their dinner, sat down in the wagon, and Kuděj swung the twig once, twice, thrice: they were on their way. And oops! the tavernkeeper's daughter had to follow on foot, runing to keep up with her fingers. They drove the whole night and the morning, and at noon they stopped at another tavern to have a good lunch and get some strength for the long journey.

While they sat at the full table, the tavernkeeper's wife—a big woman full of life—saw their strange wagon. She also noticed the girl glued to the golden balls. "She's about to steal them," thought the woman. She ran out, picked up a broom, and set after the thief!

But what happened? The broom stuck to the girl's back. Not only that: the woman's hands stuck to the broom handle as if they were carved from one piece of wood. She had to stay there.

The travelers finished their lunch, seated themselves in the wagon, and took off. The girl and the woman had to run behind.

The next morning Kuděj stopped the wagon at another tavern for breakfast. While they were eating, a farmer with a pitchfork walked into the tavern yard.

"What are you doing loafing here, you lazybones?" he bawled at the two women.

When neither one would respond, he took his pitchfork and poked the woman in the side with its handle. But hardly had he done that, when the pitchfork and the farmer as well stuck to the women.

Now the tavernkeeper had a goat, a really mean one. When the goat saw the strange farmer in the yard, he lowered his head and butted him fiercely with his horns. But he struck the farmer only once, for when he tried to pull back and attack the others, that mean goat found his horns stuck to the farmer's backside.

When the travelers returned to the wagon, all four prisoners had to run behind them to keep up. The wagon just flew along as though on wings. It was a wild ride and the hangers-on could barely catch their breath.

They went on and on until they came to a big, big city. Everyone in the place was sad. The people walked around with their heads bent. No one spoke or smiled. Kuděj was puzzled. He stopped the night watchman and asked him what all the gloom was about.

The man told him, "It has been long years now since we all grew heavy-hearted. Our King has a daughter so beautiful that you couldn't find her equal in the whole world, but she hasn't laughed once since she was born. She's drowning in melancholy and withering away. Our good King is despondent and he doesn't know how to help the poor Princess."

Kuděj listened to the watchman and then headed with his companions to the King's palace.

There he drove the wagon back and forth under the palace windows. The wheels made a horrible racket on the pavement. The Princess may have been sad, but she was curious too. She looked out the window. The moment she saw the wagon with its procession behind it, she started giggling. And the longer she looked, the funnier the scene seemed to her. The Princess could no longer contain herself: she burst into wild laughter.

The King and the Queen laughed for joy and from seeing the wagon with its curious tail of hangers-on. The tears of laughter streamed down their cheeks. They laughed and laughed until they were all exhausted. Even then, gasping for breath, they giggled and avoided one another's eyes as well as the scene outside the window. They were afraid of bursting into laughter all over again.

When the King had recovered enough to speak, he sent for the young wheelmaker and asked him where he came from. Kuděj told him all about his journey, but he was clever enough to keep the story about the magic twig to himself.

"Do you know, young man," asked the King, "what I promised to the man who could make my daughter laugh?"

No, the wheelmaker's son didn't know.

"Well," the King said, "I promised him my daughter." He sighed. "I promised him my daughter and the whole of my kingdom," he went on morosely. "I promised him my daughter, my kingdom, and my crown."

"Oh, thank you," Kuděj began, but the King interrupted him.

"Of course, I will honor my promise, but first you have to accomplish one task."

"What task?"

"It isn't that hard." The King smiled in a friendly manner. "If you can eat thirty loaves of bread and drink thirty buckets of milk, the Princess is yours."

The young wheelmaker scratched his ear. Thirty loaves, you say, he thought, and thirty buckets of milk. "Well," he said, "one has to have something to wash down such an awful lot of bread. I'll try."

He said that because he was a brave young man. And also because he remembered the fat little man and thought he might be of help here.

The royal bakers kneaded the dough and heated their ovens. Soon the servants started carrying enormous fresh-smelling loaves of bread into the young man's room and piling them along the walls. They also brought thirty big buckets of white milk. Then the King locked the wheelmaker inside his strange prison.

After sunset, the beggar with long legs and the little fat man came and stood under Kuděj's window. The tall man lifted the small one on his shoulders and pushed him into the window while the wheelmaker pulled on the other side. Then the newcomer started to eat. That was a sight to behold: the young wheelmaker only tossed the huge loaves into his friend's mouth and poured the milk after them. Before midnight struck, all the food was gone. The young man didn't have time to save a slice of bread for himself. It was quite a struggle before they managed to push the little man out the window, and it was quite a thump when they did.

When morning came, bringing the King to the door, Kuděj complained that he was starving. Astonished, the King ordered a loaf of bread and a bucket of milk to be brought to the young man; and he apologized for the fact that these were the last in the castle.

But the King thought that a husband with such an appetite and of such humble birth would not be good enough for his daughter. He decided to give the young suitor yet another task.

"There is a deep well a thousand miles away from here," the King said. "The water in the well is cold, fresh, and crystal clear. If you can bring me a flask of that water in one hour, the Princess is yours."

All right, promised the wheelmaker, he would bring the water. He didn't dally but ran to his long-legged friend.

The beggar took the flask and set off speedily. In five minutes he was at the well. He filled the flask and was about to start back when he thought, "I have enough time to rest and gather strength for the long run." He lay down to take a nap.

A quarter of an hour passed, and then another, but the long-legged messenger was still nowhere to be seen. The young wheelmaker started to worry. He found the man with the golden balls and asked him whether he could throw the balls all the way to the well.

"Why not?" said the man. "Perhaps I can throw them even farther than that."

He picked up one ball, aimed, and threw. The ball flew too far. He threw another one. This time the ball fell in the well. But the long-legged beggar did not wake up. The man took aim carefully, threw the last ball, and this time hit the messenger in the leg. The sleeper understood the hint, picked up the flask and the three golden balls, and ran back in time before the hour struck.

The happy wheelmaker brought the flask to the King, but his joy didn't last long. The King had yet another task up his sleeve.

"I have a dozen hares and three does. If you can graze them for three days without losing any of them, I'll give you the Princess. Mark that this is the last task I am giving you."

Well, Kuděj certainly appreciated that, but the promise didn't

cheer him. He knew what he was up against, and his friends said they couldn't help with this last task.

For who could have helped? As soon as they crossed the town, the hares and does darted away in all directions. The young wheelmaker could holler and call and scout around as much as he wanted, but it was all in vain.

He saw his hopes of marrying the Princess fading away, so he sat down on the ground and started to cry.

He cried and cried.

All of a sudden, the thin old man appeared in front of him, the good old man who had given him the magic twig.

"Why are you crying so?" the thin old man asked.

Kuděj told him about the hares and the does, how they had dispersed in the field and forest, and about the wonderful reward he was losing because of them.

The good old man took pity on the young wheelmaker.

"Here, take this whistle," he said. "If you blow the whistle, the herd will assemble again and follow you wherever you go."

The lad thanked him and they parted. Then Kuděj tried the whistle. He had scarcely blown it when the hares and does gathered in front of him. Filled with joy, he grazed his herd until the evening. He sang merry songs and felt as good as a king.

The next day he led the herd to the pasture again. But in the meantime, the King held council with the Queen to decide how to outsmart the clever herdsman.

"There is a strong chest in my room," the Queen said. "Let's disguise our daughter as a beggar woman and send her to buy a hare from the young scoundrel. She'll lock it in the chest, and the rascal will never be able to bring them all together."

Of course, the wheelmaker didn't want to sell, and as the Princess tried everything to talk him into it, he recognized who she was.

"Well," he said, "if you need a hare that much, I cannot say no. I will sell you one if you climb that old oak over there and sing for me."

The Princess was about to refuse haughtily, but then she remembered that she had to get the hare at any price. She climbed the tree, seated herself on a limb, and sang.

The lad was amused and he sold a hare to the disguised Princess. She locked it in her chest and hurried toward the castle. She was nearly there when the wheelmaker whistled. The hare heard him, broke out of the chest through the top, and joined the herd.

The Princess arrived home in tears.

"The hare got away," she complained, "just as I reached the gate. Look at that chest! I still can't believe it. He jumped right through the heavy oak boards. And I had to climb a tree and sing like a bird. I'll have a fit."

At that moment Kuděj entered the castle with the whole herd.

"Are they all here?" asked the King with a frown.

"Oh, yes," answered the lad. "But I tell you, you have strange birds in that forest behind the pasture. I saw one singing today, and that bird was big like . . . like . . ."

The door slammed as the Princess got up and left suddenly.

"Enough," said the King. "We'll see tomorrow."

Kuděj wasn't afraid of the next day. In the morning he drove the herd to the pasture and he didn't care where they went. He had his whistle.

It wasn't long before a raggedy woman with unkempt hair came along. But strangely enough, she carried a brand new iron chest.

"Sell me a hare, good lad, please, please, sell a hare to an old woman," she whined.

Kuděj saw that the Queen herself came in disguise. He let her beg for a good while before he said, "I'll sell you a hare for a price, but you have to dance around the herd for an hour. If you jump high enough, the hare is yours."

The Queen didn't like the idea at all, but what could she do? She didn't want her daughter to marry the son of a wheelmaker. Not even such a handsome one. She gathered her petticoats and danced. Kudĕj clapped his hands and laughed, tears streaming from his eyes. The hour was soon over, but it seemed an eternity to the Queen, who was drenched with sweat. She was breathing so hard that she just plopped on the ground and watched impassively as Kudĕj picked up a big fat hare by its ears and placed it in her new iron chest.

When she had recovered a little, she locked the chest with three heavy locks and dragged her feet back to the castle. She had crossed the bridge and was entering the gate when Kudĕj blew his whistle. The hare tore through the side of the chest and dashed over the bridge.

"Catch him! Catch him!" hollered the Queen. Two guards barred the hare's way, but the fat animal just knocked them to the ground and was gone.

When the King heard what had happened, he decided to try and outsmart the wheelmaker himself. He gave orders for a double chest to be made immediately, with brass and steel walls. Then, disguised as an ancient beggar woman, he headed toward the edge of the forest.

Well, when Kudĕj saw the third beggar woman hobbling across the field with a big steel chest, he thought it must be the King's grandmother. In fact, it took a while before he recognized who was in that disguise, such a good actor was the King. Once he saw who the raggedy hare-buyer was, Kudĕj let him beg all the more. Then he finally agreed to sell one of the hares, but, said Kudĕj,

"You will have to catch him yourself. Of course, if you catch a doe," he added, "I will give you a hare for free."

The King was about to slap the young man's face and call the guards, but then he remembered who he was supposed to be and kept his mouth shut.

Kuděj lined up the hares and does, let the King choose a spot right behind them, and then he whistled. The animals flashed in all directions and the King rolled on the grass as he threw all his weight where a hare had been just a second before. Kuděj laughed and laughed.

As fat as he was, the King darted toward a doe that was watching him curiously. He tripped on the sod, skidded on something in the grass, and sprawled again. Panting, he got up and ran after the doe, who only now judged the King's efforts serious enough. She trotted away. The hare hopped in front of the King as if to laugh at him.

The King ran and then rolled after the hare. In short, he tumbled and lurched, slipped and slid, dropped and rolled more than he ran.

Kuděj kept laughing. After an hour of this, he decided that the fat monarch had sweated enough. He whistled. At once all the animals and the King sped toward him.

"Open the chest, beggar," Kuděj ordered. Picking up the nearest hare, he tossed it inside the chest and dropped the lid. The King grabbed the chest and locked it with twelve keys. Although he was still moaning and groaning from his exertions, he turned and headed toward his castle as fast as he could go.

As soon as he had entered the courtyard, the King ordered that the bridge be drawn and the gates closed. Then he rushed into the castle. He closed and bolted the inner gate and was about to bar and lock the heavy door to the Queen's room behind him when

Kuděj blew his whistle. At that moment the hare jumped out, tore through the double wall of the chest, through the heavy door of the Queen's chamber, and through the inner gate of the castle. His last leap carried him all the way through the outer gate and the drawbridge and over the moat. There the fat animal rolled over, not unlike the King earlier that afternoon, and disappeared.

Upon hearing the crash, the Queen hurried in. She saw the peculiar hole in her door and knew immediately what had happened.

"I won't give our daughter to that brute," she exclaimed. "Let's send her away."

And so they did. They sent her to a castle beyond a large river. When the young wheelmaker reported the accomplishment of his last task, the King told him with a sad face, "Bad tidings, dear Kuděj. The Princess has vanished and we are so distressed that we don't even know where or how to look for her. If you can find her, she's yours. However, it is my personal advice that you return to your village."

The young wheelmaker was discouraged by the King's words. He walked away through the broken castle gates. In a meadow nearby he sat down and cried bitterly.

There his friends found him. Once they understood his tearful explanation, the one with the golden balls said, "Let me look in my golden balls." He looked and saw the Princess. "There is a mountain beyond the forest, a valley beyond the mountain. A large river flows through the valley. On the other side of the river stands the King's castle. In that castle the Princess is hidden. Hurry up, swim or row. I can't help you; I am afraid of water."

"I, too," said the tall beggar quickly.

"I can't swim, I've never learned. There are no lakes or rivers in my country," said the small fat one in a worried voice.

"Let's go!" was Kuděj's only answer.

They all sat in the cart. Kuděj swung the twig once and the wagon moved forward. He swung a second time: the wagon sped along smoothly. He swung a third and fourth time and the wagon spurted toward the forest edge in a cloud of dust.

Soon they reached the large river. As Kuděj had his tools along, he distributed them to his friends and they quickly built a little boat. The lad ordered the others to watch his wagon while he rowed to the castle. When he reached the stairs descending to the bank, he tied the boat to a mooring and ran as fast as he could. The Princess sat at her window. As soon as she saw Kuděj, she happily ran to meet him. She understood that she had teased him long enough and by now she was quite overcome by his cleverness and persistence.

The young wheelmaker led her down the stairs to the river, sat her on a dry seat in the boat, and rowed back to the other side. There they got in the wagon and Kuděj swung the twig once, twice, thrice . . . so many times that they could hardly hold onto the wagon, it was going so fast.

They reached the royal castle in no time. When the King saw Kuděj had overcome the final obstacle, he knew at last that no prince would have made a better son-in-law. The King felt sorry for having tormented the lad so much. He decided to reward the young wheelmaker royally and to treat him like his own son. He kissed Kuděj and at that moment all the bells in the city started to chime.

The King and Queen prepared such a magnificent wedding that the people of the country haven't stopped talking about it to this day. In time, the wheelmaker's son became King. The reign of Kuděj I was just and wise. He loved his Queen and lived with her happily until his death.

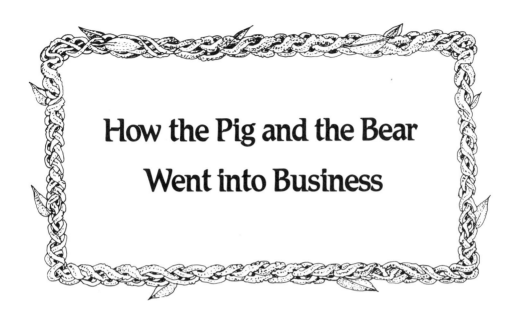

How the Pig and the Bear
Went into Business

THE PIG AND THE BEAR decided to go into business. "We'll make lots of money!" they thought.

The pig baked a bushel of potatoes and the bear fried a heap of doughnuts.

They went to the marketplace early in the morning to get the best spots. Nobody was around yet. The morning was clear and chilly. The bear had a nickel in his coat. After a while he went over to the pig's stand to warm up a little.

"How much for a potato?" he growled.

"A nickel for you."

The bear was about to say that he'd just wanted to ask, but then he changed his mind. He fished for the nickel in his fur, took the biggest steaming potato in his paws, and crossed the road back to his stand.

The business is moving, rejoiced the pig. But there were no more customers for a while, and he hadn't eaten since they started at dawn, so he crossed over to the bear's stand and bought himself a black raspberry doughnut for a nickel.

The bear was happy to make his first sale. He felt he should eat something before the customers started to flock to his stand. So he went over to buy another baked potato. The move brought him luck. He had hardly finished eating when the pig was over for another doughnut.

Then the business slacked off again until the bear bought a potato. Soon the pig was over again and the bear went right back with him to his stand to spend the earned nickel. The pig returned for a doughnut and soon they were going back and forth until they had sold everything.

They counted the money, but, strangely, the bear had only a nickel and the pig had nothing at all. They couldn't believe it.

"We have sold all our merchandise," they kept saying, "but we have no money."

In vain they counted and recounted: they had only a nickel between them after the whole day of busy trading.

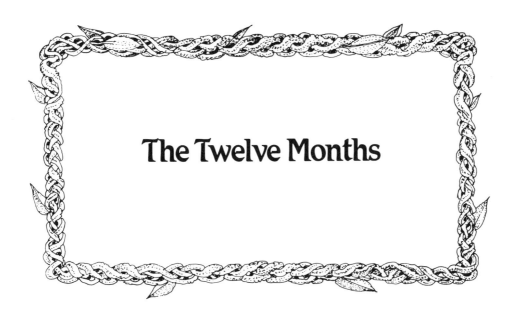

The Twelve Months

MARUŠKA LIVED IN A SMALL COTTAGE in the mountains. Ever since her father had died, her stepmother hadn't had a kind word for her and had made her do all the dirty work in the household. Her stepsister didn't have to work at all. She woke up at noon, and Maruška, who had been on her feet since dawn, was obliged to serve her breakfast in bed. Then Holena would pass the whole day preening, powdering her face and trying on clothes.

One winter day, Holena developed a sudden craving for strawberries.

"Maruška!" she cried. "Where are you, you lazybones? Fetch me some wild strawberries from the forest!"

"But sister, there's snow all over the ground, where could I—"

Note: Maruška is pronounced *marushka*.

Maruška began, but then her stepmother croaked, "Why don't you get a move on? Bring us some strawberries right away if you don't want to learn what a beating is!"

The poor girl knew only too well what a beating was. Resigned to her fate and shivering in her thin jacket, she went out into the snow, without knowing which way to turn her steps. The short winter day was fading into night, but she walked on and on over the hills, until to her surprise, she saw a faint glimmer of light far ahead among the trees.

Pressing on, she came to a forest glade. In the middle was a small fire, and around the fire twelve men were sitting on slabs of granite.

"Men of good will, please, allow me to warm my hands at your fire."

"Go ahead and warm yourself," said the white-bearded man who sat on the highest stone holding a mighty cudgel. "But what are you doing all alone in the mountains on such a cold night?"

"I am looking for wild strawberries," answered Maruška.

"Don't you know that you have to wait until June for strawberries?" rasped the old man.

"Of course I know it. But my sister and stepmother promised me a beating if I don't bring some back with me."

"Hmm," growled White Beard. He sounded like a gust of the North Wind in Maruška's ears.

"Brother June," he said to a young man sitting on one of the smallest stones on the other side of the fire, "come over and tend the fire for a while."

The young man took the mighty cudgel from him, seated himself on the highest stone, and waved the cudgel over the fire. The flames jumped up in a roaring bonfire. The surrounding snow began to thaw, and as it melted, the grass sprang up from the ground in bright green shoots and buds swelled on the bare branches. In the next instant strawberries bloomed in the grass, dropped their petals, and the first fruit reddened like little rubies among the leaves.

"Quick, Maruška, gather them up," cried the young man.

Jolted out of her bewilderment, Maruška started picking the red berries. When her pitcher was half full, the old man stood up.

"You have enough. Now head for home, quickly," he told her.

Hardly had Maruška time to breathe, "Thank you very much, men of good will," when the old man was already stirring the fire with the cudgel. The flames diminished again as she ran toward home, and snow again shrouded the forest.

Back at the cottage, her stepmother and Holena didn't offer a single word of thanks. Instead, they snatched the pitcher out of her hands and sent her to clean the pigsty. Maruška didn't get to taste one strawberry herself.

A couple of days later, Holena remarked that she'd like to smell a bouquet of violets. She told Maruška to go and pick some for her in the forest.

In vain Maruška tried to reason with her. This time Holena and her mother threatened her with the worst beating of her life if she didn't bring them what they wanted.

Again Maruška headed across the mountains wherever her feet carried her. And again she came to the little fire in the forest glade.

"Now what are you looking for in the snow?" grunted the old man with the cudgel in his hand.

"Violets," said Maruška with bated breath.

"Don't you know it's winter?" bellowed White Beard.

"Yes, I do, but my sister and stepmother will beat me terribly if I don't bring them a bouquet of violets."

The old man lowered his brow. He said, "Brother May, come over and tend the fire for a little while."

The young man next to the one called June stood up to take the cudgel and the highest seat.

When he waved the cudgel over the fire, the flames rose and the snow melted all around. The birds started to sing in the budding trees, the grass shoots appeared, and soon the meadow was sprinkled with violets.

"Gather them up, girl!"

Maruška didn't wait to be told twice. She began hurriedly to pick the flowers. When she had collected a small bouquet, the old man returned to his place and reached for the cudgel. She thanked him and headed home as the snow started to cover the mountain again.

Of course, she was put to work as soon as she entered the door, while her stepmother and her sister Holena snatched the bouquet out of each other's hands to breathe in its fragrance.

It wasn't long before Holena fancied something new.

"Get up, you lazybones," she yelled. "Bring me some fresh apples."

"But, sister—" Unheeded went Maruška's tearful entreaties.

"Out you go," ordered her stepmother, "and don't come back without fresh apples or we'll beat you to death!"

And she stuck a basket in Maruška's hand and pushed her out the door.

What was Maruška to do? The wretched girl dragged her feet in the snow, she stumbled, she couldn't see where she was going for the tears streaming down her face.

But at last she came to the same clearing in the forest. And she told the patriarch on the highest stone that she would certainly die if she didn't bring home fresh apples.

"Brother September," bellowed the old man, frowning, "come over and tend the fire."

The flames leaped into the air as a man with a short yellow beard took over the cudgel. The snow melted before Maruška's eyes. Buds sprouted into leaves and blossoms and then began to fade. Small apples appeared on the trees; they grew bigger, they turned yellow, they reddened . . .

"Quick, Maruška, gather them up!"

Maruška shook an apple tree, but only one apple dropped into her apron. She wanted to shake the tree again, but the old man took hold of the cudgel and roared, "Begone, Maruška, you must be on your way!"

She thanked him and ran off as the twelve men and the fire disappeared in a swirl of cold brittle snowflakes.

On her return, her stepmother and Holena scolded her for bringing only one apple.

"*She* stuffed herself with apples but thought a tiny sour one would be enough for us," they said.

"But, sister, they wouldn't let me take any more. I was glad to get this one!"

"Nonsense!" cried Holena. "I will go and get a bushel of them myself."

Paying little attention to Maruška's explanation of where the magic orchard was, she dressed herself in thick furs and scarves and set off for the mountain.

After a long walk, Holena came upon the fire in the glade. She neither greeted the men nor asked for permission to warm herself, but pushed two brothers aside to stretch her hands over the flames.

"What are you looking for alone in the snow?" asked the white-bearded man curiously.

"It's none of your business, you nosy old fool. But if you must know, I'm looking for apples and I don't have time to waste on a graybeard like you. Now why don't you shut up?"

And she headed into the forest.

"Brother February," said old man December, "come over and tend the fire." One of the youngest brothers, a boy with icy gray eyes, took his place and waved the cudgel over the fire. The flames dropped down until they were almost extinguished, and soon a blizzard enveloped the forest.

The storm lasted three days. On the fourth day the stepmother wrapped herself in furs and went into the mountains to look for Holena. Nothing was ever heard of them again. But that winter people heard a pack of wolves howling fiercely on the mountainside.

Maruška went about her work as usual. She wasn't lonely, as the cow, the goat, and the chicken had always been her only friends.

But when the thaw came and the streams, rivers, and waterfalls broke through their frozen armor and ran singing down the valley, something made her stop working now and then and look toward the mountain and dream. She didn't even know what she was dreaming about.

And maybe she married before the apples reddened in the orchards. And maybe she didn't marry at all. Who knows? Ask the old blacksmith's wife, she's the biggest gossip in the village.

The Firebird

THERE MIGHT HAVE BEEN or there might not have been, there was a King. He had a magnificent garden with an apple tree that grew golden apples. Every morning one blossom bloomed on the tree; by noon the petals had dropped, in the evening the apple grew, and in the morning it would have ripened.

Would have: for even though the guards steadfastly watched the apple, knowing it was as precious as the King's eye, no apple was ever found in the morning. One day, the King called his sons together and asked them for help.

"The one who catches the thief," he said, "will get half of my kingdom in reward."

Note: Ohnivák is pronounced *ohnivaak*; Liška-Ryška is *lishka-rishka*; Zlatohřivák is *zlatohrjivaak*; Zlatovláska is *zlatovlaaska.*

The eldest son said, "I will do it."

That night, armed with a crossbow and tempered darts, he went into the garden and sat beneath the tree to watch the apple. An hour passed quietly and then another. The Prince's head began nodding on his chest and shortly before midnight he was fast asleep. At sunrise, the tree was bare.

Well, the second son said he would try to catch the thief. He prepared in the same manner as his brother had, but he also was overcome with sleep by midnight. In the morning he swore he had been wide awake the whole night.

"I didn't see a living soul," he said. "The apple must have disappeared by magic."

After that, the youngest son offered to try his luck, but his brothers mocked and sneered at him as usual. His father said, "Dear child, you are too young and unwise, how could you succeed where your brothers have failed?"

The youngest Prince wouldn't give up. In the evening he armed himself with a crossbow and put the best tempered darts in his quiver. He also chose a spot under the tree and sat down, but he put a hedgehog hide over his knees.

By midnight the Prince started nodding, but whenever his head fell on his knees, the hedgehog bristles pricked his face and the Prince would wake up. Yet he didn't see the thief. It was close to dawn when he heard a faint rustling in the branches. He looked up, and tears welled in his eyes. The first sunrays were reflected in the golden apple and mirrored from a bird whose feathers glowed like fire. The firebird was picking at the golden stalk with its beak.

The Prince pulled the string of his crossbow and aimed well with a tempered dart. The death messenger whistled through the cool air. For a moment the Prince felt sorry for the fiery bird—

but the dart only brushed its wing. Before the Prince could aim a second dart, the glowing bird disappeared, leaving the apple behind. Only one feather fell slowly through the fresh air, floating back and forth like a pendulum. It seemed the golden feather would never reach the ground.

Finally the Prince reached up, plucked the feather from the air, put it in his pocket, and stretched out on the ground to catch up on the sleep he had missed . . .

The entire court was crowded around him when he awoke. His father looked at the youngest Prince sadly while his brothers laughed.

"Is that any way to keep guard?" they said.

"Look at the tree first," said the youngest son, and he showed them the golden feather and told them about his vigil. His father's pleasure was as great as his brothers' humiliation. Their envy changed to ill-hidden hatred when the King named his youngest son chief keeper of the royal gardens.

From that day on, the youngest Prince was the target of his brothers' anger. He couldn't ask his father for help, for the King's heart was taken with longing for the firebird. His growing melancholy killed all the joy in his life. Not even the golden apples could cheer him. It wasn't long before he became seriously ill. The royal physicians couldn't help him. They declared that only the singing of the firebird, Ohnivák, could cure his ailment.

Once again the King called his sons and asked them to go out into the wide world and find Ohnivák, the golden-feathered bird, for him.

"Whoever finds the firebird and brings him to me," he said, "will get half of my kingdom now, and when I die he will become King."

The Princes saddled their horses, armed themselves with their swords and crossbows, and taking a good provision of money and food, they set out. The two older brothers rode side by side, the youngest behind. At a crossroads they parted, taking separate highways. They were to meet there again in a year and a day.

As the oldest one went on along the road, a ginger vixen, Liška-Ryška, crossed his path. The Prince pulled the string of his crossbow and had aimed his best tempered dart when the vixen spoke to him in a human voice: "Spare me, good lad, and you won't be sorry."

But the Prince let the string go. The tempered dart whistled through the air. Liška-Ryška jumped up and *Phffeet!* she disappeared. The Prince's dart struck a rock and split into thousands of pieces.

The second son also met the vixen and shot at her, shattering his best dart. Liška-Ryška ran away unharmed.

When the youngest son met the red vixen, he aimed a tempered dart at her. But when she asked him to spare her life, the Prince let his arm fall. He put away the dart and released the string of the empty crossbow.

"You have saved your best dart," said Liška-Ryška, "and gained a good helper in the bargain. If you listen carefully to what I have to say, you'll get Ohnivák the firebird for your father, and more for yourself. Now follow me."

And Liška-Ryška jumped up, flipped in the air, and off she ran. The young Prince could hardly keep up with her.

Over the hills and dales she went, smoothing the trail. She leveled the hills with her bushy tail, filled the valleys, spanned rivers with bridges to ease the Prince's way. They rode over a quarter of the world and came to a brass castle. In front of the castle, Liška-Ryška stopped.

"You have to get Ohnivák alone," she said. "But listen carefully to what I have to say. Go into the castle at the stroke of noon. All the guards will be asleep. In the first chamber you'll see twelve black birds in golden cages. In the second chamber are twelve white birds in wooden cages. But you must go straight to the third chamber, where Ohnivák will be sleeping on his perch. There will be two cages by him: a golden one and a wooden one. But mind you, don't touch the golden cage or the firebird will wake up. Put him in the wooden cage or you won't fare well."

The Prince went in through the open gate. He saw everything as Liška-Ryška had described. The guards, courtiers, servants— all were fast asleep. In the third chamber, he found the bird nodding on his perch; nearby were the two cages.

He picked up the wooden one, but as he was about to put the bird in, he thought, "To the golden bird belongs the golden cage." He set the wooden cage down and reached for the golden one. But the moment he put Ohnivák inside the cage, the bird awoke with a piercing cry. The birds in the first two rooms responded in strident voices. Everybody woke up; the guards rushed in, seized the Prince, and led him to their King.

"Put the thief to death!" ordered the King.

"I am not a thief, I came to catch a thief," replied the Prince. He told the King about the golden apples, his father's illness, and what he needed the firebird for.

The King didn't comment on the stolen apples, but he said, "You can have the bird for your father if you bring me Zlatohřivák, the horse with the golden mane."

The Prince agreed and the guards took him to the main gate where they released him with a good push.

He fell at the paws of his friend the vixen. Liška-Ryška wouldn't listen to any excuse.

"I know what happened," she said. "I will help you to get

Zlatohřivák the horse, but listen carefully to what I have to say. Now follow me."

Lyška-Ryška went over the hills and dales, leveling the hills with her bushy tail, filling the valleys, building bridges to ease the Prince's way. They rode over a quarter of the world. This time Liška-Ryška stopped in front of a silver castle.

"Go into the castle at the stroke of noon," she said. "The guards will be sleeping. In the first stable you will find twelve horses as black as ravens. They will have golden bridles. In the second stable will be twelve horses white as fallen snow with leather bridles. Zlatohřivák the horse will be asleep at his trough in the third stable. But mind you, when you bridle the horse with the golden mane, don't put the golden reins on him, use the plain leather ones."

The Prince found everything in the castle as the vixen had told him. But when he put the leather reins on the horse with the splendid golden mane, he suddenly thought, "To the golden horse belongs the golden bridle." The moment the gem-studded golden reins touched the horse's neck, however, the animal started to neigh, rear, and buck so wildly that the Prince was glad when the guards surrounded him and led him away.

Their King insisted the young thief should die, but when the Prince told his story, the King pitied him and said, "I will give you Zlatohřivák the horse if you bring me Zlatovláska, the golden-haired Princess." Then he made a sign to the guards to show the intruder the way out.

When the Prince landed in front of Liška-Ryška, the ginger vixen said, "I know what has happened. I will help you again, but please, listen to what I have to say. When we come to Zlatovláska's castle, you'll find her and everyone in the castle fast asleep. Next to Zlatovláska's bed you'll see two veils, one golden and one plain.

Wrap the plain one around her and lead her out of the castle. However, if you put the golden veil on her head, the whole castle will wake up and you'll have to rely on your own wits."

Liška-Ryška jumped and ran, leading the way as before. They rode over a quarter of the world. When they came to a golden castle in the middle of a black sea, they parted.

The Prince entered the castle and found everything as Liška-Ryška had told him. Forgetting his purpose, he stood motionless for a long time, admiring the sleeping maiden's beauty. Her hair shone so bright that tears welled up in his eyes. Finally the Prince remembered Liška-Ryška's advice. He wrapped the plain veil around Zlatovláska's body. But as he was leaving the room, he thought, "To the golden hair, the golden veil belongs."

Well, he was dragged before the Sea Queen the moment he touched the golden veil. The Queen wanted to hand him over to the hangman, but when the Prince told his story, she said, "Of course you should die for your impudence, but the execution can wait. If you perform three tasks, I will give you my daughter. If not, you will be beheaded."

The Prince agreed.

"The first task," said the Sea Queen, "will be very easy. You must drain all the water from the lake behind the palace garden. I will send you your tool tomorrow."

The Prince was worried, but it wasn't until the next day that he saw how desperate his situation was. The Queen sent him a little golden sieve to transport the water in. He spent the greater part of the day trying to haul the water in the sieve, but the work was all in vain. The sun was declining in the west when the Princess happened by. They talked for a while and when she was about to leave, Zlatovláska said, "You don't seem to know how to go about your task, let me help you a little."

And before the Prince could respond, she took the sieve and tossed it into the middle of the lake. The water began to churn and boil, and before the sun touched the horizon, the lake was dry.

The Queen didn't seem all that happy that the task was fulfilled, but she only said, "We'll see how well you'll fare tomorrow. I want you to remove the mountain that blocks the sunshine from coming into my bedroom window."

The Prince started digging at the foot of the mountain at dawn, but one could hardly see the little trench he had dug by the late afternoon. He was catching his breath when a bright light dispelled the shadow of the mountain: Zlatovláska came by, just by chance. When they had talked for a while, she offered to help, and to his astonishment, she took a pin and a buckle out of her hair and tossed them to the ground. The pin started digging and the buckle shoveling. Before the night fell, the ground below the Queen's windows was level as a dance floor.

"By the way," said the Princess, "tomorrow you may have to choose me from among my sisters. If you watch closely, you'll see a fly circling around my head. That's how you'll recognize me."

The shadow of the mountain seemed to have stuck to the Queen's face when she came to examine the accomplished task. She said briefly, "Tomorrow you'll have to pick out Zlatovláska from her sisters. If you can do it, she's yours. If not, you will be shorter by your head."

The Prince didn't think that would be a difficult task.

"How could I miss that golden hair?" he thought.

He slept quietly for the first time in three days. But the next morning when he entered the throne room, he knew he had been judging the task prematurely. Twelve maidens sat on twelve stools in the large chamber. All were dressed in white, and all wore white headdresses that completely covered their hair. Looking at their faces, the Prince suddenly realized he had never noticed the color of Zlatovláska's eyes. He had been so dazzled by her golden hair. He paced desperately around the sisters, examining their faces, when he was distracted by a buzzing sound. Presently he saw a fly circling one pretty face. He looked closely. The eyes were blue.

"This is she," he said, "this is the bride I want!"

Well, the Queen didn't like it, but she gave him her daughter, and off they went on the Prince's horse. Liška-Ryška ran behind them, striking down the bridges with her bushy tail, digging the valleys and building the hills.

When they came to the castle where Zlatohřivák the horse lived, Liška-Ryška said, "I know how you feel. You have become accustomed to each other, and it's hard to part. Leave Zlatovláska outside. I'll go with you in her likeness. Then you can exchange me for the horse and ride on as fast as you can. I'll take care of the rest."

She jumped up, flipped in the air, and turned into a woman, so much like Zlatovláska that the Prince could hardly tell them apart.

He led her to the castle. The King was delighted and he gave the young man Zlatohřivák, the horse with the golden mane, and as much gold as he could carry. He asked the Prince to stay for the wedding, but the Prince said he was eager to see his ailing father immediately. Zlatovláska joined him at the edge of the forest and they sped away.

In the meantime, the King offered a splendid dinner to honor the golden-haired maiden. Beaming with delight, he asked his courtiers how they liked her. They all praised her beauty.

Suddenly one of the courtiers said, "Isn't it strange that such a beautiful woman should have such foxlike eyes?"

At that moment, the girl jumped up, flipped in the air, and turned into the ginger vixen again. She was off before the courtiers and the King could close their mouths. She caught up with her friends, striking the bridges as she ran, digging the valleys and building high hills with her bushy tail.

Before they had reached the next castle, Liška-Ryška changed herself into a horse with a golden mane: none could have told the one from the other. The Prince led her to the castle and exchanged her for Ohnivák the firebird. Once the Prince was on his way, the King showed the horse to his wife.

"What a strange horse," she said, "with a fox's tail!"

Liška-Ryška jumped in the air, regained her own likeness, and ran away. With her bushy tail she struck the bridges, dug valleys, and built hills. When they came to the place where they had first met, Liška-Ryška said, "Now I must leave you. But listen carefully to my last advice: *Do not buy meat from the gallows.*"

With these words she jumped, flipped in midair, and ran away into the woods.

The Prince returned to the crossroads where he was to meet his brothers. He was surprised when he saw two gallows poles erected there. A procession of people was coming from the nearby town, headed by two men in chains.

To his astonishment, the Prince recognized his two brothers. They had gambled in a tavern, he learned, until they lost all their money, horses, weapons, and much, much more. Now they were to be hanged, for they could not pay their debt. The Prince forgot all that he had suffered from his older brothers and paid their debt from his store of gold. He bought them new horses and clothes befitting their rank, and he armed them with new swords and crossbows.

That night, the three Princes pitched their camp only one day's

ride from their father's palace. But when the youngest was sound asleep, the two rescued brothers took their new swords and cut him to pieces.

They threatened to kill Zlatovláska in the same way if she told anybody about the murder. The eldest brother took her and the middle one took Zlatohřivák the horse. They shared the gold evenly.

When the old King heard about their approach, his health improved, and all the more so when he saw the beautiful horse and his daughter-to-be. But Ohnivák the bird wouldn't sing, Zlatohřivák the horse wouldn't eat his fodder, and Zlatovláska would not comb her golden hair. At this the King took to his bed, more ill than ever before.

In the meantime, Liška-Ryška came to the ditch where the two brothers had left the cut-up body of the youngest Prince. She knew what had happened. She ran around sniffing until she found a crow's nest in the thicket. Carefully she took the two newly hatched birds into her teeth.

The crow mother cawed sadly, "What did they do to you, to deserve such a horrible end?"

"I won't kill them," said Liška-Ryška, "if you bring me water from the Source of Life and the Source of Death."

The crow picked up two fish bladders in her beak and flew without delay to the end of the world. There she filled the two bladders with water from the Source of Life and Source of Death. Then the crow returned to the vixen and deposited the two bladders in front of her.

"Now, give me my children!" the crow said.

Instead, Liška-Ryška tore the young birds in half. Heedless of the mother crow, who cawed and threatened to peck out her eyes, the vixen spilled a little Water of Death on the torn bodies.

The halves united again without a scar. Then the vixen spilled a little Water of Life on the bodies, and the young crows started crying and asking for food.

Liška-Ryška didn't wait to hear the mother crow's thanks but ran back to the ditch where the murdered Prince lay. She spilled a little Water of Death on the cut-off limbs, and the parts united to form one body. Liška-Ryška spilled a little Water of Life on the dead body, and the Prince awoke, rubbing his eyes.

"I have slept for a long time," he said.

"And you wouldn't have awakened if it weren't for me," said Liška-Ryška. "Now you have to do me a favor. Pick up your sword and cut off my head."

The Prince didn't want to do anything of the kind, but finally he agreed. With a heavy heart he let his sword fall on the vixen's slender neck. The ginger head flew off but there was no blood, and a handsome young man appeared in front of the Prince.

"Thank you, my savior," said the man. "I am the brother of your wife. Now let's go to your castle to regain what properly belongs to you."

The Prince walked for four days before arriving at the castle. On the way he exchanged his clothes with a beggar. He hid his sword and crossbow under the rags and dirtied his face.

He went to the palace gate begging for food. They sent him to the stable to wait for some leftovers. As the disguised Prince entered the stable, Zlatohřivák the horse whinnied happily; he started to eat his fodder. In the King's room, Ohnivák the bird began to sing, and in her bedroom, Zlatovláska started to comb her golden hair. The King felt suddenly twenty years younger, and he jumped out of his bed to greet his future daughter. But when the oldest son asked the King for his royal blessing, Zlatovláska said, "This is not my husband; my husband is the one who can make Ohnivák sing, Zlatohřivák eat his fodder, and my heart dance."

The oldest Prince pulled out his dagger to thrust it into her heart. But the beggar ran into the room, drew a sword from under his rags, and cut off his head. The middle brother ran out and into the stable, but Zlatohřivák the horse reared and bucked, and kicked so hard that the Prince's skull cracked open.

The youngest Prince married Zlatovláska soon afterward and became King, keeping his father with him for a long, long time, until the end of his days.

Krakonoš

IN THE HIGH MOUNTAINS of Bohemia there once lived many giants, but today only one is left. His name is Krakonoš, and he is also a powerful magician who can take many forms. And what a moody giant he is! When he frowns, clouds cover the tops of the hills; and when he swears, the thunder rolls down the valleys. He is ancient and, like the old of the world, he angers easily. Stinginess and falseness he particularly loathes. This is one of the true stories about Krakonoš.

Once there was a poor widow who lived in the village of Rokytnice. One market day, she had only three eggs from her hen and nothing left in her larder. She didn't feel like trudging the long way down to the valley's marketplace. But when she asked

---

Note: Krakonoš is pronounced *krakonosh*; Rokytnice is *rokitnitze*; Jablonec is *yablonetz*; Lysá Hora is *lisaa hora*.

her neighbors to lend her a few pounds of potatoes, they only laughed at her. The widow saw she had no choice but to walk the four hours to town to sell her three eggs.

Not far from her cottage she met an old man on the road. He was walking in her direction, but he panted heavily, wheezed noisily, and stopped every dozen steps to rest. As the widow passed him, he called after her, "Mother!"

She stopped where she was and hollered back, "What is it?"

"Would you please give me something to eat? I haven't had a morsel in my mouth since Thursday."

"I have nothing," said the widow, "nothing but these three eggs I must sell." And she turned to go.

"Mother," called the old man again, "would you give me one, please?"

The widow thought a bit and said, "No, no, I cannot do that." She began to stride resolutely down the road. But she had walked only a dozen steps before she stopped and headed slowly back.

"Here you go," she told the old man, handing him an egg. "How in the world you're going to eat it, I don't know. Goodbye."

She had walked for five minutes when again she heard, "Mother!"

She could hardly believe the old man's voice could carry so far, but when she turned around, she was astonished to see him walking only some twenty paces behind her.

"Mother," he said, "I just wanted to thank you for the egg. It was delicious."

"You're most welcome," said the woman, "but now I must—"

"I wonder if you could give me another one," the old man interrupted. "The first egg only whetted my appetite."

The widow sighed deeply and looked away to the valley behind Rokytnice River, as though there hovered there a world of interest. Then, with another sigh, she pulled a second egg from her pocket and handed it to the old man. She looked up the road where she lived, and then down the road where she was going, looked up and down again, and finally began to walk back home.

"Mother!" She heard the old man who was again close behind her.

"What now?" she said.

"I just wanted to thank you for the eggs. Delicious," said the old man.

"You're welcome," she answered, walking on.

"By the way," he said, "there is a third egg, isn't there?"

"What about it?"

"I wondered whether maybe you'd sell it to me."

"I just might do it."

"How much is it?"

"Listen, old man, you might as well name your own price. But let's pretend you're paying me for all three eggs."

"Well," said the old man, "I thought I'd give you three golden ducats for the last egg. But you're the boss, so here's a ducat for each egg. Thank you, mother." He took the egg from her and in an instant was gone. Three golden ducats lay shining in the widow's hand.

On her way back the widow knocked at her neighbor's door again.

"I told you I couldn't give you any handouts," said the neighbor.

But the widow answered that she wanted to buy a bushel of potatoes and some flour and lard.

"And what will you pay me with?" snickered the neighbor.

"Why, with this ducat," said the widow. "I hope you have enough change."

The neighbor's face turned white and her mouth flew open. Then she started running about like a barnyard hen, searching for

the best potatoes, the whitest flour, and the finest lard. The neighbor burned with impatience to know where the widow's ducat had come from. It took a while, however, before she was able to put together a clear question without stuttering and faltering.

But the widow made no secret of her good fortune.

"Even before I had gone a few dozen steps toward the market," she said, "a man stopped me and bought my three eggs—and paid a ducat for each of them."

The neighbor was overwhelmed.

"Don't bother paying me now," she said. "I just remembered I have to go to town. I mean, you were right, I'll have to get change, anyway. Take the food you have here as a present from me."

The neighbor almost pushed the widow out the door, and in a jiffy had filled her wicker dosser with all the eggs she had in her house. She could hardly lift the dosser on her back, for she had filled it with well over twelve dozen eggs, but finally she managed. Bent over, with the straps cutting sharply into her shoulders, she ran out the door and down the road.

"If that beggarwoman sold her eggs for a ducat each on the road," she muttered to herself, "they must sell for much more in town. Maybe double. That would make, that would be . . . maybe two hundred ducats . . . three hundred ducats, maybe . . ."

In spite of the heavy load of eggs on her back, she was in such a rush, so eager for the ducats, that she made the four-hour trip in three.

As she neared the outskirts of Jablonec town, she heard a cracked voice cry, "Mother!"

She stopped and saw an ancient man panting behind her.

"Whadya want?" she said.

"Where are you running, in such a hurry?" asked Krakonoš, because that's who the man was.

"To the market."

"What do you sell?"

"Eggs."

"How much for?"

"Three ducats each."

"I'll give you a ducat, mother. Whadya say? Don't you want to spare yourself the trip to the market?"

The woman just snickered. "Three ducats, I said. There's a good price for you. Take it or leave it."

And she hurried toward the marketplace. There the farmers were already closing their stalls, but she opened her dosser and waited for customers. Many were still there, all looking for a bargain. A half a grosch, the smallest coin, was the best offer she got for a dozen eggs. The buyers laughed and laughed when she asked three ducats for an egg. Then she was asking two, then one. But she wouldn't sell for under a ducat.

"That is my final price," she said. The people only shook their heads and went away. When night started to fall, the woman had sold not a single egg. She could only pack the eggs and start on her way back. It took her much longer to get back to Rokytnice. Not far from her home she met the old man again.

"Hey, you there," she hollered at him. "I managed to save a few eggs and you can have one for a ducat now."

"You must be joking," the old man said. "You see this grosch? That's what I'll give you for a dozen."

The woman stared in astonishment and then began to haggle. "Surely more than that for these eggs," she said.

"No more," the old man answered.

And try as she would to wrangle more money from the man, his answer remained the same. At last, tired and distraught, she agreed to take twelve groschen in return for all her eggs.

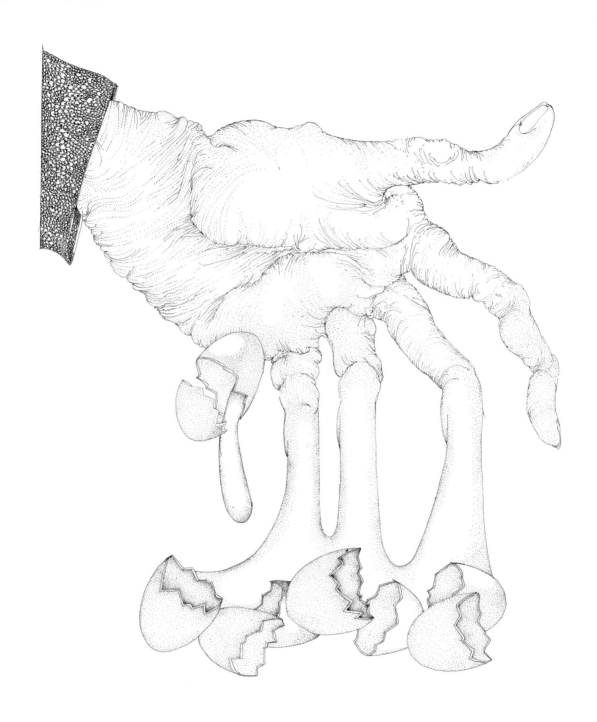

"Now, Mister Ever-so-smart, how can you carry the eggs? You have no basket of your own. Now, here is a very good dosser, worth at the very least a ducat and a half in town. But this isn't town, so let me give you my special roadway price, let's see . . ."

"I don't have to carry them anywhere," the old man said. "Just wait a second. But please, mother, by all that's holy, don't look."

With her wrinkled hands, the woman covered her eyes. The old man, Krakonoš, broke an egg. The woman peeked out and couldn't believe what she saw. Krakonoš picked a bright golden ducat from the egg's yolk, put it in his pocket, and tossed the egg to the roadside. Then he broke another egg, and inside glowed another ducat.

"One minute, one minute," the woman yelled. "These eggs, I forgot, I promised to give them to a neighbor. Good sir, let me have them back."

And the woman argued a full five minutes before she convinced Krakonoš to take his money back. As she returned the twelve groschen he had paid her, she told him, "Keep the two eggs you've already broken."

Krakonoš left and she hardly waited to see him go before she picked an egg from the dosser and broke it on a stone. Inside, nothing. She broke another egg, and another. She broke all the eggs, one by one. Her hands were sticky with yolks and whites and the road was covered with shells. But she found not a single ducat, not even a grosch. She sat down amidst the eggshells, her eyes glazed, her breathing heavy.

Finally she jumped up and began to kick the basket until it lay in pieces. As she turned toward home in despair, she heard a magnificent laugh thundering high above Lysá Hora, the Bald Mountain.

"Krakonoš," she whispered in awe.

ABOUT THE AUTHOR

Born and brought up in Czechoslovakia, Vít Hořejš now lives in New York City where he is involved in a number of theater projects. He has written original scripts and performed both in the U.S. and abroad with Ta Fantastika Black Light Theatre (Company) and the Divadlo Theatre, of which he was a co-founder. He has given numerous performance-readings of folk tales in libraries and other institutions, such as The Metropolitan Museum of Art in New York City. Mr. Hořejš has long been interested in making Czechoslovak folk and fairy tales accessible to English-speaking young people; this volume is the first collection of these stories to be published.

ABOUT THE ARTIST

Jim Spanfeller is a well-known and highly regarded illustrator of more than 70 books, including such works as *Where the Lilies Bloom* by Vera and Bill Cleaver and *Dorp Dead* by Julia Cunningham. His work has received over 200 awards from the A.I.G.A. and citations from other professional associations. Mr. Spanfeller has been an artist all his life and says, "My only interests are drawing, reading, and talking a lot." He frequently collaborates with his son Jim, Jr., a writer and the publisher of *Newsweek on Campus.* Mr. Spanfeller lives with his wife Pat in Katonah, New York.

J 398 H   48709
Horejs, Vit.
12 iron sandals & other
Czech folk tales $11.95

DISCARD

S-2/14   LU-6/13   2 circs   14 libs